Jane Austen

The Pride & Prejudice Colouring Book

Featuring
Original Illustrations
by C.E. Brock

All rights reserved. No part of this publication may be reproduced, distributed, or transmitted in any form or by any means, or stored in a database or retrieval system, without the prior written permission of the publisher.

It is a truth universally acknowledged, that a single man in possession of a good fortune, must be in want of a wife.

"*I hope Mr. Bingley will like it, Lizzy.*"

"She is tolerable: but not handsome enough to tempt me; and I am in no humour at present to give consequence to young ladies who are slighted by other men. You had better return to your partner and enjoy her smiles, for you are wasting your time with me."
Mr Bingley followed his advice. Mr Darcy walked off; and Elizabeth remained with no very cordial feelings towards him. She told the story however with great spirit among her friends; for she had a lively, playful disposition, which delighted in anything ridiculous.

"She is tolerable; but not handsome enough to tempt me."

"Pride", observed Mary who piqued herself upon the solidity of her reflections, "is a very common failing I believe. By all that I have ever read, I am convinced that is is very common indeed, that human nature is particularly prone to it, and that there are very few of us who do not cherish a feeling of self-complacency on the score of some quality of other, real or imaginaary. Vanity and pride are different things, though the words are often used synonymously. A person may be proud without being vain. Pride relates more to our opinion of ourselves, vanity to what we would have others think of us."

"'If I were as rich as Mr. Darcy, I would keep a pack of foxhounds, and drink a bottle of wine every day.'"

"Indeed, Sir, I have not the least intention of dancing. I entreat you not to suppose that I moved this way in order to beg for a partner." Mr Darcy with grave propriety requested to be allowed the honour of her hand; but in vain. Elizabeth was determined; nor did Sir William at all shake her purpose by his attempt at persuasion.

"*Mr. Darcy, you must allow me to present this young lady to you as a very desirable partner.*"

Jane had not been gone long before it rained hard. Her sisters were uneasy for her, but her mother was delighted. The rain continued the whole evening without intermission; Jane certainly could not come back.

'Jane had not been gone long before it rained hard.'

Had she found Jane in any apparent danger, Mrs Bennet would have been very miserable; but being satisfied on seeing her that her illness was not alarming, she had no wish of her recovering immediately, as her restoration to health would probably remove her from Netherfield.

'*Neither did the apothecary think it at all advisable.*'

Elizabeth took up some needlework and was sufficiently amused in attending to what passed between Darcy and his companion.

"*You write uncommonly fast.*"

Elizabeth, having rather expected to affront him, was amazed at his gallantry; but there was a mixture of sweetness and archness in her manner which made it difficult for her to affront anybody; and Darcy had never been so bewitched by any woman as he was by her. He really believed, that were it not for the inferiority of her connections, he should be in some danger.

"*No, no; stay where you are. You are charmingly grouped.*"

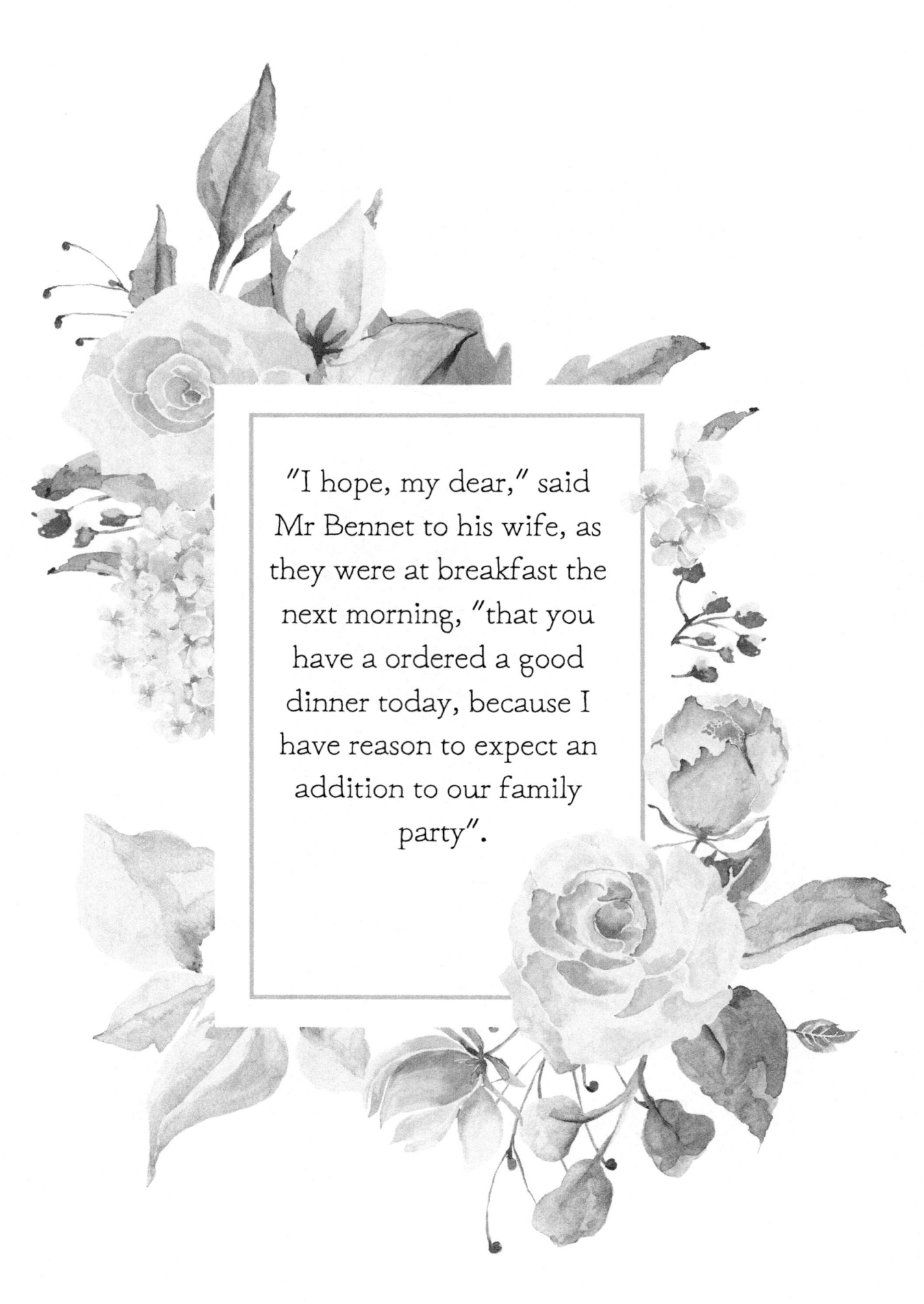

"I hope, my dear," said Mr Bennet to his wife, as they were at breakfast the next morning, "that you have a ordered a good dinner today, because I have reason to expect an addition to our family party".

'"Why, Jane—you never dropped a word of this—you sly thing!"'

Mr. Bennet's expectations were fully answered. His cousin was as absurd as he had hoped, and he listened to him with the keenest enjoyment, maintaining at the same time the most resolute composure of countenance, and except in an occasional glance at Elizabeth, requiring no partner in his pleasure.

'Lydia interrupted him.'

Lydia's intention of walking to Meryton was not forgotten; every sister except Mary agreed to go with her; and Mr Collins was to attend them, at the request of Mr Bennet, who was most anxious to get rid of him, and have his library to himself;

'Mr. Denny entreated permission to introduce his friend.'

Mr Wickham was the happy man towards whom almost every female eye was turned, and Elizabeth was the happy woman by whom he finally seated himself;

'It was over at last, however. The gentlemen did approach.'

To Elizabeth it appeared, that had her family made an agreement to expose themselves as much as they could during the evening, it would have been impossible for them to play their parts with more spirit, or finer success;

'Prefaced his speech with a solemn bow.'

"I do assure you, Sir, that I have no pretension whatever to that kind of elegance which consists in tormenting a respectable man. I would rather be paid the compliment of being believed sincere."

'"Almost as soon as I entered the house I singled you out as the companion of my future life."'

"From this day you must be a stranger to one of your parents. Your mother will never see you again if you not marry Mr Collins, and I will never see you again if you do."

'"You must come and make Lizzy marry Mr. Collins."'

Miss Lucas perceived him from an upper window as he walked towards the house, and instantly set out to meet him accidentally in the lane.

'*Love and eloquence.*'

"So, Lizzy" said he one day, "your sister is crossed in love I find. I congratulate her. Next to being married, a girl likes to be crossed in love a little now and then. It is something to think of, and gives her a sort of distinction among her companions."

'The first part of Mrs. Gardiner's business was to distribute her presents'

"But these things happen so often! A young man, such as you describe Mr Bingley, so easily falls in love with a pretty girl for a few weeks, and when accident separates them, so easily forgets her, that these sort of inconstancies are very frequent."

'On the stairs were a troop of little boys and girls.'

When Mr Collins could be forgotten, there was really a great air of comfort throughout, and by Charlotte's evident enjoyment of it, Elizabeth supposed he must be often forgotten.

'Mr. Collins and Charlotte were both standing at the gate in conversation with the ladies.'

When the ladies returned to the drawing-room, there was little to be done but to hear Lady Catherine talk, which she did without any intermission till coffee came in

'To scold them into harmony and plenty.'

"I shall not say that you are mistaken," he replied, "because you could not really believe me to entertain any design of alarming you; and I have had the pleasure of your acquaintance long enough to know, that you find great enjoyment in occasionally professing opinions which in fact are not your own."

"You mean to frighten me, Mr. Darcy."

"My dear Eliza, he must be in love with you, or he would never have called on us in this familiar way."

"*You must allow me to tell you how ardently I admire and love you.*"

Mr Darcy's letter, she was in a fair way of soon knowing by heart. She studied every sentence; and her feelings towards its writer were at times widely different.

"Will you do me the honour of reading that letter?"

Elizabeth could not see Lady Catherine without recollecting, that had she chosen it, she might by this time have been presented to her, as her future niece; nor could she think, without a smile, of what her ladyship's indignation would have been.

'I assure you I feel it exceedingly.'

These two girls had been above an hour in the place, happily employed in visiting an opposite milliner, watching the sentinel on guard, and dressing a salad and cucumber.

"Look here, I have bought this bonnet."

She lost all concern for him in finding herself thus selected as the object of such idle and frivolous gallantry; and while she steadily repressed it, could not but feel the reproof contained in his believing, that however long, and for whatever cause, his attentions had been withdrawn, her vanity would be gratified and her preference secured at any time by their renewal.

'*He looked surprised, displeased, alarmed.*'

Every idea that had been brought forward by the housekeeper was favourable to his character, and as she stood before the canvas, on which he was represented, and fixed his eyes upon herself, she thought of his regard with a deeper sentiment of gratitude than it had ever raised before; she remembered its warmth, and softened its impropriety of expression.

'She stood several minutes before the picture, in earnest contemplation.'

Whilst wandering on in this slow manner, they were again surprised, and Elizaeth's astonishment was quite equal to what it had been at first, by the sight of Mr Darcy approaching them, and at no great distance.

'The introduction was immediately made.'—

"There is also one other person in the party," he continued after a pause, "who more particularly wished to be known to you. - Will you allow me, or do I ask too much, to introduce my sister to your acquaintance during your stay at Lambton?"

'Bingley entered the room.'

She was wild to be at home - to hear, to see, to be upon the spot, to share with Jane in the cares that must now fall wholly upon her, in a family so deranged; a father absent, a mother incapable of exertion, and requiring constant attendance; and though almost persuaded that nothing could be done for Lydia, her uncle's interference seemed of the utmost importance, and till he entered the room, the misery of her impatience was severe.

'She eagerly communicated the cause of their summons.'

She has been allowed to dispose of her time in the most idle and frivolous manner, and to adopt any opinions that came in her way.

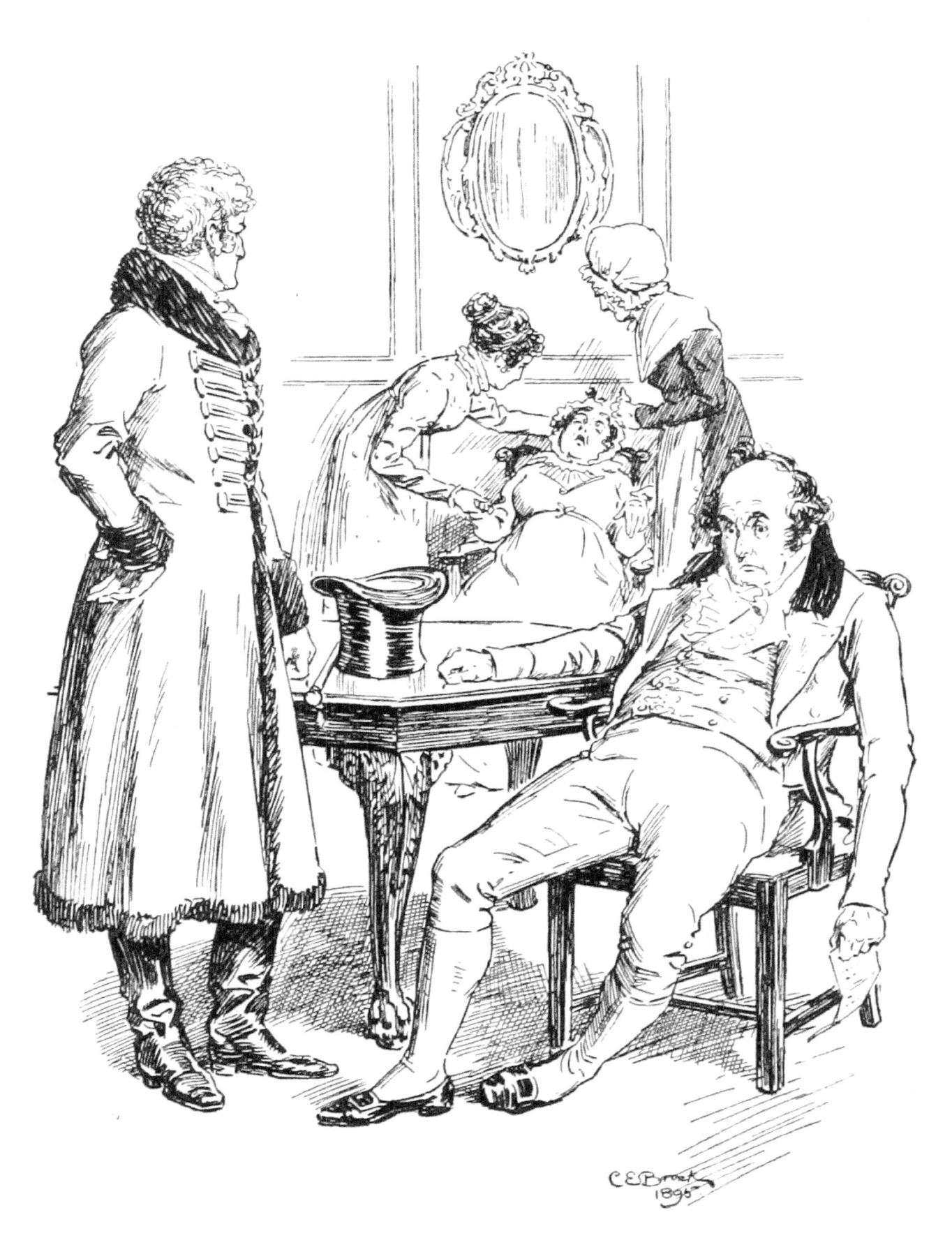

"I never saw any one so shocked."

"She had better have stayed at home," cried Elizabeth; "perhaps she meant well, but, under such a misfortune as this, one cannot see too little of one's neighbours. Assistance is impossible; condolence, insufferable. Let them triumph over us at a distance, and be satisfied."

'"Oh, papa, what news? what news?"'

"I thank you for my share of the favour," said Elizabeth; "but I do not particularly like your way of getting husbands."

'She went after dinner to show her ring and boast of being married to Mrs. Hill and the two housemaids.'

Wickham was not at all more distressed than herself, but his manners were always so pleasing, that had his character and his marriage been exactly what they ought, his smiles and his easy address, while he claimed their relationship, would have delighted them all.

'She held out her hand.'

His behaviour to her sister was such, during dinner time, as showed an admiration of her, which, though more guarded than formerly, persuaded Elizabeth, that if left wholly to himself, Jane's happiness, and his own, would be speedily secured.

'She perceived her sister and Bingley standing together.'

Elizabeth's congratulations were given with a sincerity, a warmth, a delight, which words could but poorly express.

'*Mrs. Bennet was privileged to whisper it to Mrs. Philips.*'

"While in their cradles, we planned the union; and now, at the moment when the wishes of both sisters would be accomplished, in their marriage, to be prevented by a young woman of inferior birth, of no importance in the world, and wholly unallied to the family!"

"Miss Bennet, I insist on being satisfied."

At night she opened her heart to Jane. Though suspicion was very far from Miss Bennet's general habits, she was absolutely incredulous here.

'All was acknowledged, and half the night spent in conversation.'

During their walk, it was resolved that Mr Bennet's consent should be asked in the course of the evening. Elizabeth reserved to herself the application for her mother's.

"'Now, be sincere; did you admire me for my impertinence?'"

He could even listen to Sir
William Lucas, when he
complimented him on
carrying away the brightest
jewel of the country

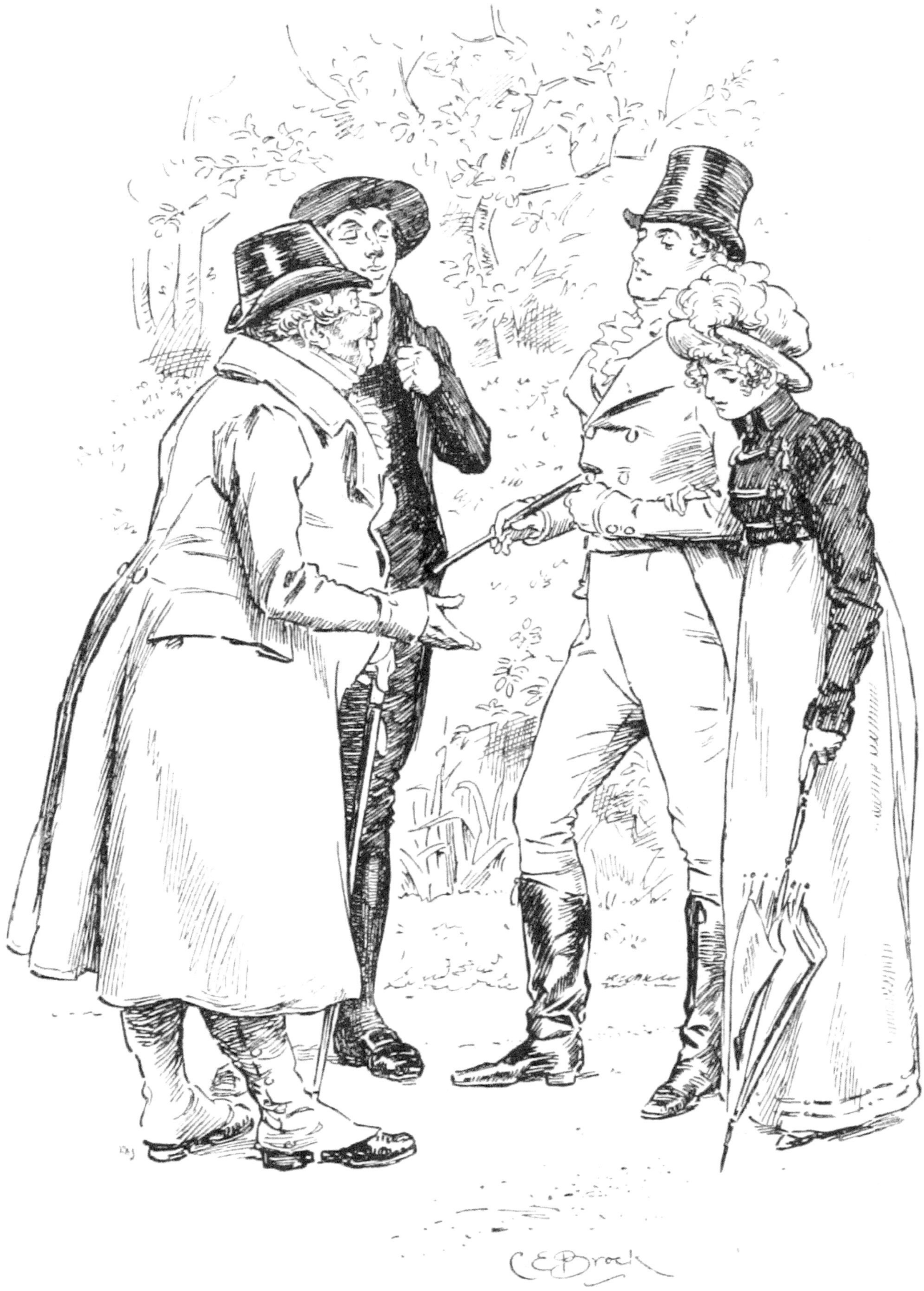
C.E.Brock

She looked forward with delight to the time when they should be removed from society so little pleasing to either, to all the comfort and elegance of their family party at Pemberley.